stories from rainbow

Collins   Glasgow and London

Introduction

"Rainbow," Thames Television's programme for young children is shown to viewers throughout Britain and is widely acclaimed as the most lively show produced for three to six year olds.

Everything included in the programme is carefully designed to be simple enough for the young viewers to enjoy. One of the most popular

Thames Television's Rainbow is produced by Charles Warren.

moments is when "Rainbow's" own storybook is opened.

Here, then, are stories from "Rainbow", complete with the original bright illustrations used on television. Children who watch the programme will be fascinated to hear some of their favourite stories again, and as stories are regularly repeated on TV this fun will continue.

Even children who have never seen "Rainbow" will greatly enjoy the stories because they are short and simple and planned around familiar actions and objects.

Contents

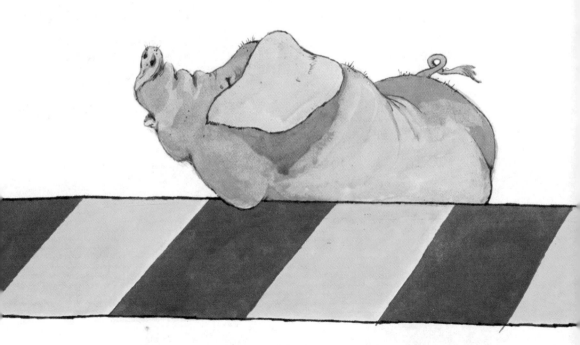

Little pig's wish

by Bridget Appleby

The smallest pig was unhappy. He didn't like the shape of his nose. "It's horrible!" he squealed. "It's just like a dinner-plate! It's a rotten old nose!"

His mother spoke to him gently. "It's a very nice nose, littlest pig. It's exactly the right shape for the job it has to do."

"What job?" grunted little pig.

"Well, if it wasn't that flat shape you couldn't dig in

the hard ground and grub up the acorns and roots that
you like to eat."

But piglet didn't believe her, and went on
grumbling. He grumbled right up until bedtime.

"It's an *awful* nose! How can anyone say it's a nice
nose! I *wish* I had a nose like an elephant! Wouldn't that
be smashing! Now that's what I *call* a nose! . . . ."

And he fell asleep thinking of how smashing it
would be to have a nose like an elephant.

The next morning he awoke to the sound of all his brothers and sisters laughing. When he opened his eyes he saw that they were laughing at *him*.

"Look at your nose!" they all gasped, rolling about on the straw.

"It's all long and thin! It's an *elephant's* nose!"

And so it was. Littlest pig had wished himself an elephant's nose!

"Just what I wanted!" he said to everybody.

"This is what a *real* nose should look like! Let's all go out to the orchard and dig for breakfast."

But when he tried to root about in the earth like the other piglets, he found that his new nose wasn't quite so marvellous. Smallest pig kept tripping over it and getting branches and roots tangled in it. The nose didn't seem to do the things he wanted it to do. Once it even got tied into a knot!

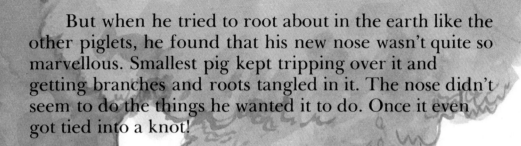

"This is terrible!" thought little pig in a panic. "I can't dig up any food at all! I shall starve . . ." and great big tears started to trickle down his new nose.

"Well, what did I say!" said Mother Pig, who had come up quietly behind him.

"Your old nose might have looked like a dinner

plate, but it was just right for a little pig, wasn't it?"

Little pig sadly agreed with her.

"Never mind," said his mother. "I think perhaps tomorrow you'll wake up and find your very own nose back again."

I wonder if he did?

Sports day at the pond

by Mary Campbell

Ferdie Frog sat on a waterlily leaf in the middle of the
pond, and wrinkled up his nose. He was thinking — and
he always wrinkled up his nose when he was thinking.
Tomorrow was going to be Sports Day in the pond
where he lived, and he wanted very much to win a prize.
But he didn't know yet which prize he would go in for.

Because he was a frog and had very long, strong,
back legs, which made him very good at jumping, he
could win easily the jumping prize. But Ferdie wanted
to win a different prize. Above all the things he could do
he loved to sing — or croak, as some people would call
it. He didn't see why he shouldn't try to win the prize
for the best singer — the crown of buttercups.

He sat on his leaf and watched all the other creatures of the pond practising for the sports. The fish were twisting and turning for the swimming races — the ducks were seeing who could stay with their heads under the water the longest. Some dragonflies were skimming along the top of the water like speedboats, and a crowd of butterflies were practising their flying relay race.

Ferdie knew that as a frog he had a very good chance of winning the jumping competition, but he won that prize last year, and this year he wanted the singing prize. Deep down in his broad froggy chest he longed to be asked to sing with the Croaking Choirboys, famous for miles around as the best frog singers.

On the morning of the sports — a happy Ferdie put his name down for the singing and climbed onto the platform with the other singers: blackbirds and nightingales, thrushes and warblers; there was even a duck who sang a comic song and made everyone laugh. Then, just as a blackbird was about to finish a very pretty song, came Ferdie Frog's turn, and he was clearing his throat, ready to start his song, when a great shadow fell over him.

He looked up — to see an enormous bird coming straight at him. But it wasn't a singing bird — it was a heron, and herons eat frogs for breakfast, lunch and

dinner. But before the heron could gobble him up,
Ferdie made a great jump into the air, and landed on
the ground. Then he jumped again . . . and again . . .
and again. He went on taking great jumps right up into
the air until the heron flew away.

Suddenly he found himself in a circle of other frogs, all clapping and croaking because he had jumped higher and longer than anyone else in the long-distance jumping competition.

So for the second year running he had won the jumping prize. He also made up a special croak song against herons, and that night he sang it to a crowd of admiring frogs who jumped up and down with delight.

Mouse finds out

by John Kershaw

Mouse found a shed at the bottom of the garden and in
he scampered. He was very hungry and very tired. A
man with a big machine had knocked down the house
he'd always lived in and the people there had gone away

without leaving any bread or cheese for Mouse to eat.

He was so hungry. He jumped on to a bench. And what do you think he found? An old sandwich. He ate it up, very quickly. That made him feel better though he was still tired. Then he saw, near the edge of the bench, a plastic flower-pot.

Now Mouse had never done any gardening in his life and he didn't know about flower pots — so he went up to it and sniffed curiously. Perhaps he could eat it, too. But even his sharp little teeth couldn't bite into the pot. He sniffed again but this time he accidentally knocked the pot over. In a great fright he scampered

away to hide behind a trowel. Nothing else happened, so he crept back to the pot and peered inside.

It was quite empty. He stepped carefully in but as he began to walk about the pot started to roll over.

Out he jumped, just in time. The pot fell off the bench onto the floor. Mouse peeped over the edge. It had landed by the table leg on top of an old sack. He jumped down and crept inside again. This time the pot

didn't roll about — in fact it was quite comfortable. At last he'd found out about plastic flower-pots. "It's for me

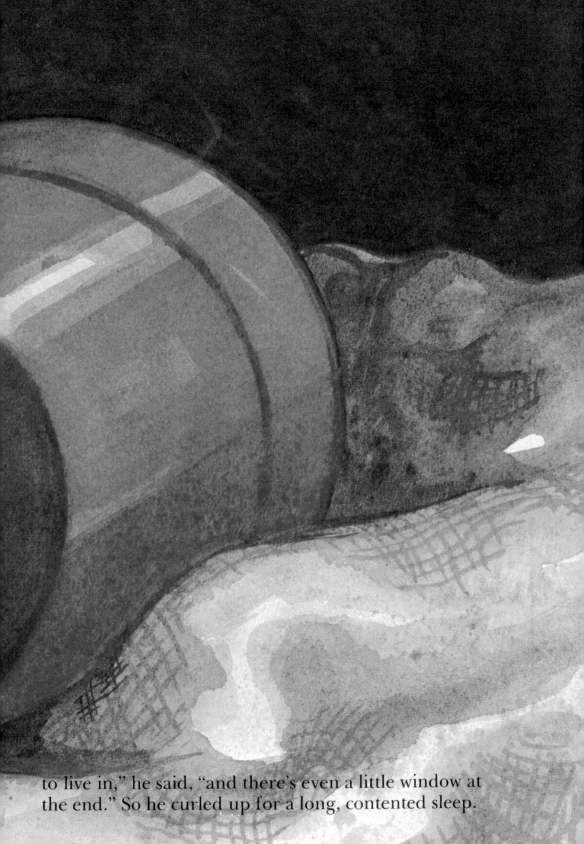

to live in," he said, "and there's even a little window at
the end." So he curled up for a long, contented sleep.

Albert Owl

by Bridget Appleby

Mr and Mrs Owl were very happy. Their two white eggs
had hatched out into beautiful baby owls, one called
Emily and the other called Albert.

   One night Mrs Owl decided it was time for Emily
and Albert to leave the nest in the hollow tree and learn
to fly. So she went to waken them up.

"Wake up Emily, wake up Albert!" she said.

Emily's eyes opened but Albert's eyes stayed tightly shut.

"Why isn't Albert waking up?" Mrs Owl asked Emily.

"Oh, he always sleeps at night," said Emily. "And he stays awake in the daytime. He says the daylight keeps him awake."

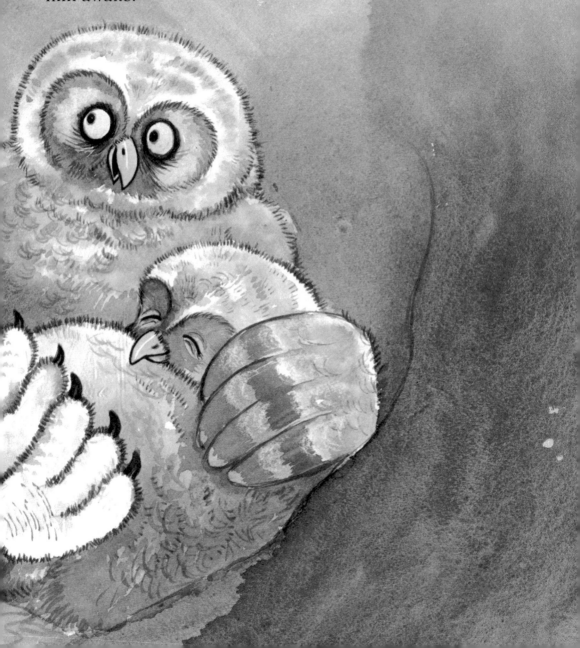

Mrs Owl went to talk to Mr Owl. They were very worried, because as you know owls are not like children — they sleep in the daytime and are awake at night.

"We must find a way of making Albert sleep during the day so that he isn't tired at night," decided Mr Owl. So that is what they tried to do.

Mr Owl found a handkerchief which someone had

dropped, and he fixed it up over the hole to shade the nest inside and make it dark. But Albert didn't sleep. He said the spots on the hanky were so pretty that he stayed awake looking at them.

Mrs Owl made some dark patches out of two walnut shells to cover Albert's eyes. But Albert didn't sleep. He

said he wouldn't wear them because Emily laughed at him. Mr Owl asked two woodpigeons to come and sit outside the nest, hoping that their soft "coo-cooing" would lull Albert to sleep. But Albert didn't sleep. He said how could he sleep with that awful noise going on outside.

By night-time, Albert *was* ready to sleep, and Mr and Mrs Owl had given up.

"You will just have to come to the flying lessons, sleepy or not," said Mr Owl. "And if you fall off a branch, well, it might waken you up!"

So out into the treetops they all went, Mr Owl, Mrs Owl, Emily, and finally, half-asleep Albert.

"All right Albert," said Mr Owl, firmly. "Open your eyes and watch."

Albert's eyes opened. And when they did they opened very wide indeed, for he saw the big white moon and the sparkly stars for the first time.

"Isn't night-time BEEautiful!" he cried. "From now on I'm going to sleep in the daytime so that I can stay awake to see the moon at night. I'm *never* going to sleep at night again!" And he never did.

Sam the goat

by John Kershaw

Sam was a young goat. He lived on a farm with his
mother, some sheep and cows, and an old horse called
Jerry. Sam loved chasing things. His mother was always
saying, "Can't you walk about quietly, like Jerry the
horse, instead of jumping and charging at everything?"

But Sam wasn't interested in walking about quietly. Whenever he saw anything that moved he wanted to run after it. He chased birds and rabbits and cats; he even charged through hedges.

Sam was always in trouble for breaking the gate and knocking things over. So his mother went to see Jerry the horse. "He won't stop rushing and jumping up and down," she said. "And he never looks where he's going. Can you help me?" The old horse said he would think about it.

Next day Sam saw Jerry standing in a corner of the field. He laughed to himself. "There's old Jerry. He looks half asleep to me. I think I'll go and waken him."

Sam leapt over the farmyard fence and began charging towards the horse as fast as he could go. Jerry watched him carefully, out of the corner of his eye. He

waited and waited, standing quite still. Then, at the very last moment, as Sam was almost up to him, he moved out of the way.

Sam had his head down, so he didn't see Jerry move. Instead, he ran on. Splosh! Straight into the middle of a big patch of mud. It took him a long time to clean himself but it was the last time he tried chasing Jerry. After that Sam walked slowly round the farm with his head up, looking very carefully to see where he was going.

Michael and Jimbo

by John Kershaw

This is a story about Michael and his little black dog, Jimbo. Jimbo the little black dog belongs to Michael, and usually he sleeps curled up in a round basket in the kitchen. When Michael comes down in the morning to take him for a walk, Jimbo jumps out of the basket and runs round and round the kitchen with excitement.

When they reach the field Jimbo runs round and round there, too.

Michael watches from the middle of the field laughing at the fun and frolics of the little black dog.

But sometimes Michael has to stop watching because he becomes dizzy as he turns round and round to watch Jimbo running round in circles.

Sometimes when the weather is fine Michael's
mother takes both Michael and Jimbo to the children's
playground in the park.

Michael goes on the swings and Jimbo runs
backwards and forwards, barking.

Then Michael has a ride on the little roundabout
and Jimbo chases round and round after him.

Once they went for a walk in the wood. It was full of fallen twigs and branches that crackled when you trod on them. Michael thought it exciting to jump on the twigs and make them crack. And Jimbo thought it very exciting chasing round and round the trees with twigs in his mouth.

When Jimbo is excited he wags his tail from side to side and up and down. And when he's very very excited he twists it round and round, like the sail on a windmill.

At night, when it's time to go to bed, Michael lies
down flat on his face and goes to sleep.

When Jimbo goes to bed he jumps into his basket
and turns round and round until he's made a nice
comfortable space in the middle of the blanket. Then he
flops down and goes to sleep too.

And in the morning both Michael and Jimbo get up
and start all over again.

Henry and the peculiar parcel

by Bridget Appleby

Number 6A Buttercup Street was squashed between number 6 and number 8 Buttercup Street. Because it was squashed up and high instead of being spread out and low, it was very tall and had four floors and 127 stairs.

At the top of the 127 stairs lived an old man who was rather deaf and kept a canary in a cage.

Below *him* lived a lady with red hair, who never stopped talking.

Below *her* lived a little girl called Patsy, her parents, and a dog called Sunshine.

Below *them* lived Mr McArthur, who owned the house and looked after the whole building.

Lastly below *him,* down some dark dusty stairs was the dark dusty cellar, where the boiler that heated the water lived.

One day Henry the postman stopped outside number 6A. He carried a big brown parcel. He looked at the name written on the label, and it said:

"A. MOUSE, 6A BUTTERCUP ST."

"Well," said Henry, "This is 6A, but I'm blowed if I know who A. Mouse is, or which floor he lives on. I'd better start at the top and work down I suppose."

So up the 127 stairs he trudged and knocked at the door at the top.

When the old man answered it, Henry held out the parcel. "Are you Mr Mouse?" he asked.

"I wish it was," said the old man who thought that Henry had said, 'is this your house?'

"No. Try the people below."

Down on the next floor the red-haired lady opened the door when Henry knocked.

"Ooh, the postman!" she began. "A parcel for me? It must be from my niece Angela. She lives in Margate with her husband, he's a doctor, lovely man. Funny smell this parcel's got. Do you know Margate? Lovely place . . ."

When she saw the name on the label she said, "A. Mouse. That's not me. That's not my name! Must be for those people downstairs — try below. Try below."

On the floor below, Patsy answered the door.

"Hello," said Henry. "Is your daddy A. Mouse?"

"No, he isn't," replied Patsy, "But our dog's called Sunshine."

Patsy's Mum in the kitchen called out, "Try below. Try below."

So downstairs Henry stamped and rang Mr McArthur's bell. "Does A. Mouse live here?" asked Henry wearily. "I've got a rather smelly parcel for him."

"Nobody here by that name," said Mr McArthur. "And I should know."

"Shall I try below?" suggested Henry, noticing the dark dusty stairs.

"There's only the cellar below, but try if you like," Mr McArthur replied. "You might find A. Mouse down there."

So down the cellar steps crept Henry, who didn't much like the dark.

"Hello!" he whispered nervously at the bottom. "Does A. Mouse live here, by any chance?"

"Yes," called a little voice, and out from under Mr McArthur's boiler scurried a little brown — *mouse*!

"Are you A. Mouse?" Henry asked, surprised.

"Of course I'm a mouse!" squeaked the mouse. "What do you think I am, a giraffe? And that's my

parcel, I can smell it from here! It's some special cheese that my best friend has sent me. He lives in a good cheese shop. Would you like a taste?"

"No thanks!" said Henry, who wasn't partial to cheese. "I'll be going now."

So *up* the cellar steps he climbed, very glad indeed that he had safely delivered the peculiar parcel . . . and so was A. Mouse who had a lovely dinner that day.

The monkey and the tap

by John Kershaw

Someone at the zoo had left a tap running and none of the animals could sleep because the water made such a noise — splish! splash! splatter! splash! all night long.

At last the elephant said, "I'm very clever. I know what to do. I'll drink up all the water. Then there won't be any more noise." So he walked slowly to the tap, put out his long trunk, and took a long, long drink.

But the tap kept on running, splish! splash! splatter! splash!

Then the giraffe said, "I can drink more than you, elephant. I'll show you how to stop the noise." And he too walked to the tap, stretched out his long, long neck to the water, and drank and drank and drank.

But still the tap kept running, splish! splash! splatter! splash!

Then a bird with a big beak came along. It was a pelican. "I can drink more than either of you," he said. And he stretched his big wings and flew to the tap. There he opened his beak and let the water pour in. But even he couldn't make any difference.

The tap kept on running, splish! splash! splatter! splash!

Next a little monkey came along. "I know what to do," he said. "I'll soon stop the tap running."

But the other animals didn't believe him. He wasn't as big as they were, so he couldn't possibly be as clever. They just laughed at him and stood in the way so that he couldn't even see the water or the tap. But he could hear it all right, going splish! splash! splatter! splash!

"Well, I do know how to stop it," he said. And he clambered up onto the elephant's back. Then he leaned forward, stretched out a long arm, and turned off the tap. The water stopped running.

"There," said the monkey. "I told you so."

"Huh!" said the elephant, "I stopped the water by drinking so much."

"Oh no," said the giraffe, "*I* stopped the water."

"No, no," said the pelican, "I stopped the water."

But I know who really stopped the water running. So do you, don't you?

Grumps

by Anna Standon

An old man called Grumps lived in a cottage all by
himself and, as he didn't care for anyone or anything,
nobody cared for him.

One day while Grumps was out working in his
garden, some children stopped to stare at him.

"Shoo! Be off with you! Go away!" he shouted,
waving his arms angrily.

As they turned to run there was a crash! Little Jackie had dropped and broken her beautiful doll. Jackie was very upset and instead of running away like the other children, she walked right up to Grumps.

"Look what you made me do!" she cried. "You made me break Esmeralda!"

"Esmeralda?"

"Yes, my lovely doll and . . . and she's special 'cos she's so old. She belonged to my granny, and now you've made me break her, so you'll have to mend her."

Jackie thrust her broken doll into old Grumps's

hands and ran home crying bitterly. Grumps was so surprised. No one had ever spoken to him like that before.

He stared thoughtfully at the broken doll and suddenly he remembered that his sister had owned a doll just like this when they were children. Then a very strange thing happened . . . old Grumps smiled, as he remembered his sister.

"Maybe I can mend the doll," he thought, and off he went to find glue and paint to do the job.

Jackie could scarcely believe her eyes when she called for her doll. She ran to show her friends.

"Look," she said, "Old Grumps has taken such care mending Esmeralda she's as good as new."

"What *our* old Grumps?" they cried.

"Yes," Jackie nodded.

"Well," said Tommy, "I shall take him my broken steam engine. Maybe he will mend it for me, no one else can." And off he went to see old Grumps.

"Good morning," said Tommy bravely.

"Huh! what's good about it?" snorted Mr Grumps.

Tommy held out his steam engine.

"Please mend Puffing Billy for me, Mr Grumps."

"I'll see, I'll see," snapped old Grumps. And he took the steam engine and slammed his door.

Old Grumps stared for a long time at the steam engine. He said to himself, "I remember when I had one

like this, when I was a child!" And once again old Grumps smiled as he set to work, for he had always liked his steam engine and taken great care of it.

Tommy was very pleased when he collected his steam engine for it was as good as new.

He showed it to his friends. Then Bobby took his teddy which had only one eye, Lucy took her doll's house with its broken door and Johnny took his horse with its broken leg to old Grumps and he mended them with such care that they became as good as new.

Now, although old Grumps still lives by himself, he is never alone for long. The children come every day with something or other to mend, and while old Grumps works, they sit and watch and they all laugh and chat. For you see old Grumps isn't grumpy any more. He's a happy man, he cares for everyone and everyone cares for him.

Grandma Bricks of Swallow Street

by John Kershaw

Grandma Bricks keeps a shop in Swallow Street. One day a strange noise is heard coming from Grandma's shop. Someone is snoring. But it's not Grandma Bricks. She is sitting in her chair, waiting for people to come to the shop to buy things. So I wonder who is making the noise?

"Z-z-z-z." The noise comes up from a box in the corner. Why! It's Fuzzby the dog, and he's fast asleep.

"Ping!" goes the shop door and in walks Abel Jones the garage man, scratching his head. "I need a box, Grandma," he says. "I need a box to keep tools in."

Grandma Bricks thinks hard for a moment, then gets up to show Abel a work bench she has for sale.

"I don't need a bench," he says. "Just a box, to fit into an empty corner."

"This bench would fit into a corner," says Grandma.
But Abel wants a box not a bench.

Grandma finds an old frying-pan. "You could keep
tools in this," she says. "It would fit into a corner."

"A box would fit into a corner better," Abel laughs.
"Besides, I don't want to fry my tools, Grandma."

Grandma finds an old hat on the bench and tries it
on. "You could keep tools in this hat," she says. "If it was
upside down."

"No thanks," says Abel. "All I want is a box."

Just then Barney comes into the shop. Grandma tells him what Abel is looking for.

"What about an empty sack?" asks Barney.

But Abel does not want a sack, either. "It's a box I
need," he says. "A box with corners, to fit in a corner."

Abel finds a box. "This will do," he says, picking it
up. "Just what I want."

"Now where did that come from?" Grandma says.
Fuzzby jumps back into the box as quickly as he can,
barking loudly. Abel is not going to have his best
sleeping-box to keep tools in. Certainly not.

"Hello, Fuzzby," says Clare, running into the shop.
"Do you want to come to the park, to play?"
But Fuzzby is staying where he is until Abel goes.
And I don't blame him. Do you?

The cow, the pig and the tunnel

by John Kershaw

One day a farmer decided to move his farm to another
part of the country. So he sent his animals to the railway
station, to catch a train to the new place. There was a
cow called Jingle, and a pig called Snort. The animals
became quite excited as they climbed into a big truck
just behind the engine. They'd never been on a train
before. The whistle blew pree-ee-eep, the engine tooted
toot-toot and off they went.

It was all new and very interesting looking at fields
and going over and under bridges. They even went
through the middle of a big town.

Then, suddenly, they came to a hill. It was a very
steep hill and very high. In the side of the hill was a big
black hole. The cow and the pig said, "Stop little train."
So the little train stopped. "What's the matter?"
"It's that funny black hole," Snort the pig said.
"I don't like black holes," said Jingle, the cow.
The little train laughed. "That's not a black hole,"
he said. "It's a tunnel."
"What's a tunnel?" Jingle asked.

"A tunnel," said the little train, "goes right through the hill and out the other side. It's like a short cut. Instead of having to climb that steep path up the hillside, which is very hard work indeed, we go through the tunnel."

Jingle and Snort said that they didn't want to go through the tunnel, thank you very much. They didn't like big black holes. "And that *is* a black hole," said Snort, "whatever you like to call it."

The little train laughed again. "All right," he said. "You get off and climb over the hill. I'll meet you the other side."

So Jingle and Snort got off the train and began to climb. The train watched them for a little while, then tooted and trundled into the tunnel as happy as a train could be.

"It's a long way," said Jingle.

"Yes, it is," said Snort, "and I'm hungry."

"Never mind," Jingle said, "we can't go back now." So on they went. Up and up. Higher and higher until, at last, when they were tired out, they got to the top.

"Look," said Snort pointing downwards. Jingle looked. There, right at the bottom of the hill, was the little train waiting for them.

"Perhaps we should have gone through the tunnel after all," said Jingle.

"Yes, perhaps we should." agreed Snort.

The animals had a little rest, then they set off again to catch the train. As soon as they got into the truck just behind the engine they both fell fast asleep. And when

they arrived at the station, the farmer, who was waiting for them, had to wake them both up before he could take them to his new farm.

A hippo at the bottom of the garden

by Anna Standon

At the bottom of the road, at the bottom of the hill, in an old red house, lived a boy called Timothy with his mother, his father, his sister and his brother.

One day Timothy was fishing in the pool at the bottom of the garden when up popped — a hippo!

"Eh-hum, good afternoon!" said the hippo. Timothy stared.

"Eh, excuse me but aren't you a hippo?"

"That's right, I'm a hippopotamus to be precise but my friends call me Hippo."

"But . . . but do you live here?"

"Of course. You see, it's nice and cool at the bottom of the pool," said the hippopotamus.

"But I've never seen you here before," said Timothy.

"Perhaps you haven't looked hard enough."

Just then, Timothy's mother called, "Teatime, Timothy!"

"Tea!" said the hippo, "I'd like a nice cup of tea."

"Would you like to come to tea with us?"

"No, I think I'll stay here at the bottom of the garden."

"All right, I'll bring you some," said Timothy.

"Don't go away." He ran towards the house.
"Mum, there's a hippo at the bottom of the garden!"
"A hippo at the bottom of the garden?" cried his
mother, his father, his brother and his sister.
"Yes, and he'd like some tea."

"All right," said Timothy's mother. "Perhaps he'd like a bun as well?"

"Oh yes," said Timothy and took a bun and cup of tea to the bottom of the garden.

"Thank you," said the hippo and he munched the bun and drank the tea, right to the bottom of the cup. "Well, I must be going now, Timothy. See you soon. Gloo-blye!" he gurgled as he sank to the bottom of the pool where it was nice and cool.

Just then Timothy's mother and father and sister and brother arrived at the bottom of the garden.

"Where's the hippo?" asked Timothy's father.

"There!" said Timothy, pointing to the rings in the water. "Although he's gone to the bottom of the pool he said he'd be back to see us. It's so nice having a hippo at the bottom of the garden," said Timothy.

The Wotsit from Whizz-bang

by Samantha Lee

One very hot day Andy was in the garden drinking a milkshake, when suddenly he heard a strange voice coming from the cabbage patch.

"Ow!" it squeaked, and "Stop it," and "Gerrof."

Andy rushed over to the cabbages, and there was Moggy the cat holding a very peculiar something in his mouth.

"Whatever is it?," thought Andy aloud.

"I'm a Wotsit, of course," said the thing crossly.

"A Wotsit?" repeated Andy.

"Yes. A Wotsit. Are you deaf?" it squawked.

"Well! Don't just stand there while this monster eats me."

Moggy dropped the Wotsit quickly.

The Wotsit was about as tall as a large mushroom. It was round and completely covered in green, curly hair. Its many arms and legs stuck out in all directions and instead of a mouth it had a spout like a teapot.

"What're you staring at?" it asked. "Haven't you ever *seen* a Wotsit before?"

"No, I haven't," said Andy. "Where have you come from?"

"I've come from Whizz-Bang," it said, and turned a

joyful somersault. "Thank you for saving me from the monster, but I still feel quite faint."

"It was only Moggy," said Andy, "and he wouldn't hurt a fly. But perhaps you'd like a drop of milkshake to make you feel better, " Andy offered kindly.

"What is a milkshake?" asked the Wotsit.

"You know," said Andy. "It's a drink made with milk and some lovely flavour."

"Really?" the Wotsit was amazed. "What's a drink? We don't have drinks in Whizz-Bang."

"Well!," said Andy. "A drink is a liquid. Look! If I put this straw in my mouth and suck, the milkshake goes into my mouth, down my throat and into my tummy. It tastes very nice. Would you like to try?"

"Yes please," said the Wotsit, taking the beaker in its hands and putting the straw in its spout.

There was a very loud gurgling noise and lots of froth and bubbles appeared on top of the milkshake. The Wotsit jumped in alarm.

"Well, I don't think much of that," it said.

"Silly," laughed Andy, "you're blowing instead of sucking. That's no way to drink a milkshake. You have to breathe in and suck the milkshake up the straw into your mouth. And then you swallow it."

"Why didn't you say so in the first place?" said the Wotsit huffily. It took another large gulp of milkshake, then its eyes crossed and went round and round like Catherine wheels.

"I say," said the Wotsit. "That's not bad," and gulped another spoutful. Then it did four cartwheels, five somersaults and ended up balancing on one finger.

"I like it. I like it," it squeaked. "I must rush back to Whizz-Bang and tell all the other Wotsits what fun it is to drink milkshakes."

"Tell me," said Andy. "Why is the place you live in called Whizz-Bang?"

"Watch," said the Wotsit, "and I'll show you."

Then it went WHIZZZZZ-BANGGGGG, and disappeared.

The Swallow Street party

by John Kershaw

One day the people of Swallow Street thought they
would have a party — a "street" party. Luckily the

110

weather was fine. Everyone took tables and chairs
outside and they hung flags and balloons from the
windows and doorways and drainpipes. Then they sat
down to have a big tea.

After they had eaten their fill, Mr Grindle dressed up as a clown and did some party tricks with a plate. He rolled the plate along one arm, then down his leg, up his other leg, and then up his other arm. Last of all he caught the plate in his mouth. Everyone thought Mr Grindle was a very funny clown, and very clever too.

Everyone except Clare Nap. She did not think he was
funny or clever.

So Mr Grindle blew a fizzer in her face.

You know what a fizzer is, don't you? It's a bit like a
whistle. You blow into it and a long tube of paper
uncurls. Sometimes there is a feather on the end of the
tube, and it tickles people. Fizzers make a funny noise as
well when you blow into them.

But Clare didn't think the fizzer was funny either.

Next Mr Bep came forward and began to play his violin. Everyone clapped and cheered and moved the tables and chairs so that they could all dance to his music.

They did have a good time. Abel Jones, the garage man, danced with Grandma Bricks; Joey danced with Susan; and everyone danced with everyone else. Even Fuzzby had a sort of dance with Willie.

It was the best street party anyone in Swallow Street had ever been to because it went on for a long time; long after bed-time.

Willie and Susan and Joey and Fuzzby all hoped
that there would be another street party very soon.

The cockerel who couldn't stop worrying

by Bridget Appleby

Colin the cockerel was a born worrier. That means he worried about *everything*, whether it needed worrying about or not.

He worried about his six fat, white hens who fussed
and pecked around him. He worried in case they could
not lay their six eggs a day for Farmer Tree who looked
after them. "Stop worrying!" clucked Clara, the fattest
hen. "We'll lay our eggs, we always do! I don't know why
you worry so!" She was a very sensible bird and was
quite right too. They always did.

Colin worried about his chicks as well. There were ten of them, like little yellow round balls of fluffy wool on legs. He worried in case they got lost.

Most of all he worried about oversleeping in the morning. Because very early, every morning, he had to climb on top of the hen house and crow "Cock-a-doodle-doo!" as loudly as he could, to let everyone know that a new day had started. Some nights he did not go to sleep at all, just in case he couldn't wake up. And all next day he would be very tired and fall asleep counting the chicks, which was very *worrying*. "Tt . . . Tt . . ." tutted Clara. "You're making yourself poorly with all this worrying! Just you stop it before it's too late!" But Colin couldn't.

Then, one morning, Clara pointed to his feet and squawked, "What *have* you been standing in! Your feet and legs are all purple!"

Colin couldn't remember at all standing in anything purple. It was very strange and very worrying. He started to worry about his purple legs.

The next day, all the feathers on his tummy had turned purple . . . and Colin had no time to worry about his hens or his chicks. He was too busy worrying about his purple tummy.

The day after that, his wings and back had turned purple! Only the tip of his tail and his head were the right colour now!

"Oh! Oh! Oh dear!

What shall I do!" croaked Colin. He could hardly speak for worry. "All my beautiful white feathers! Whatever is the matter with me?"

"*I* know what's the matter with you!" said Clara. "You have worried so much that you've made yourself purple with it! And the more you worry, the more purple you'll get! I shouldn't be surprised if you're purple *all over* tomorrow!"

And he was. The next day he was purple from top to toe. Now he was *frantic* with worry. "What will

people say! Farmer Tree won't want a purple
cockerel! I'll lose my job! Oh dear!
Oh calamity!"

When Farmer Tree saw Colin in all his purpleness,
he couldn't believe his eyes. He called Mrs Tree and
they stared and stared. But he wasn't angry with Colin
for being purple.

Instead, he telephoned the newspapers and the
people from the television and soon there were great
crowds around the hen house, all looking at Colin. "Isn't
he lovely!" they said. "Isn't he *unusual*! What a beautiful
colour that cockerel is!"

"They *like* me being purple!" gasped Colin. "I don't have to worry about it!" and he stood up proudly, enjoying all the fuss and praise.

But as he stopped worrying, another strange thing happened. Gradually his feathers turned paler and paler until they went completely white once more, and then all the people went away, because no one wanted to look at an ordinary white cockerel!

Colin didn't mind though. He was so pleased to be himself again, and he knew that from now on, he would try to stop worrying because it didn't help things very much.